Hello Kitty®

Hello Christmas!

illustrated by Higashi Glaser

HARRY N. ABRAMS, INC., PUBLISHERS

hello snowflake

hello snowman

hello friend

hello sled

hello fun

hello mistletoe

hello sugarplum

hello treats

hello carols

hello stocking

Hello Kitty

hello trimming

hello tree

hello elf

hello toyland

hello reindeer

hello presents

Library of Congress Cataloging-in-Publication Data

Hello Kitty, hello Christmas! / illustrated by Higashi Glaser.
p. cm.
Summary: Christmastime for Kitty means snowflakes,
a snowman, carols, presents, ornaments, and more.
ISBN 0-8109-3543-0
[1. Christmas--Fiction. 2. Cats--Fiction.] I. Glaser, Higashi, ill.
PZ7 .H374453 2002
[E]--dc21
2002004997

Printed and bound in Hong Kong
10 9 8 7 6 5 4 3 2 1

Harry N. Abrams, Inc.
100 Fifth Avenue
New York, NY 10011
www.abramsbooks.com

Abrams is a subsidiary of
LA MARTINIÈRE
GROUPE

hello Christmas!

hello ornaments!

a

a

b

b

hello wonder!

c

c

d

d

1. Carefully punch out each disk along the dotted lines.

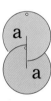

2. Slide two matching pieces together along the slotted lines, perpendicular to each other. Tape along the seams for extra stability.

3. Tie a string through the hole, decorate your tree or room!

hello trimmings!